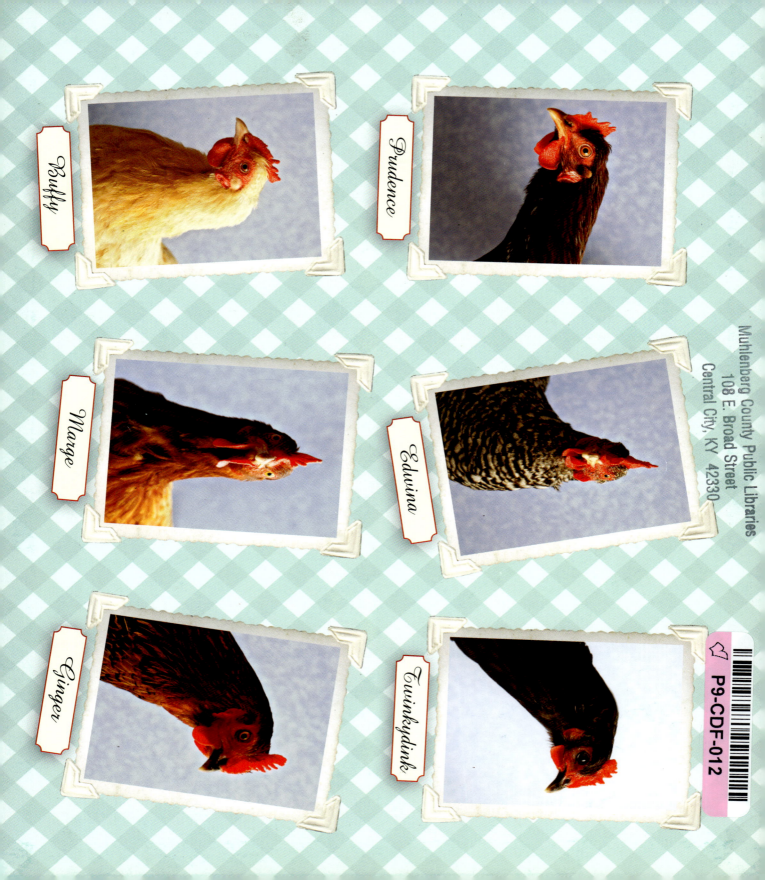

Buffy

Prudence

Marge

Edwina

Ginger

Twinkydink

TILLIE
LAYS AN EGG

Terry Golson

with photography by

Ben Fink

SCHOLASTIC PRESS · NEW YORK

In the backyard

of the big white house on
Little Pond Farm there is
a small henhouse.
Seven chickens live here.

Each hen lays one egg a day.

The hens lay their eggs in nesting boxes.
There are seven chickens but only three boxes.

What do the hens do?

They take turns.

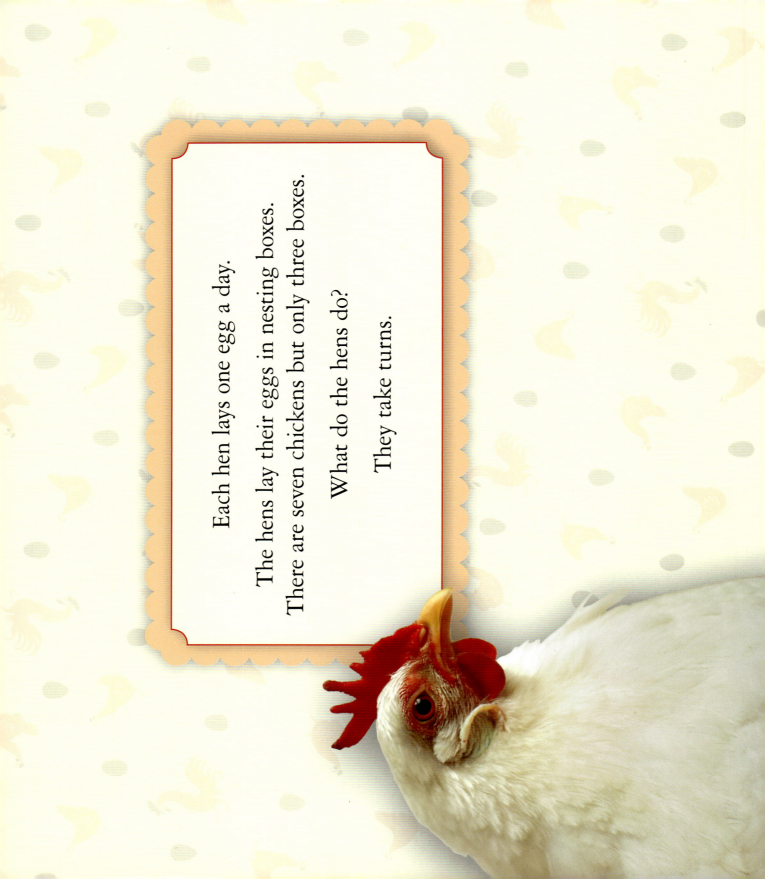

On Monday, Buffy, Ginger, and Twinkydink go first. They lay their eggs and then go outside to scratch for corn in the barnyard.

Next, Marge, Edwina, and Prudence lay their eggs, and then join their friends outside.

Now there are six eggs in the nesting boxes.

Where is Tillie?

She doesn't want to wait for her turn in a nesting box. She doesn't want to eat the corn in the barnyard. She wants to look for worms.

Yum, she thinks. *There are plenty of tasty worms here!*

Where has Tillie laid her egg?

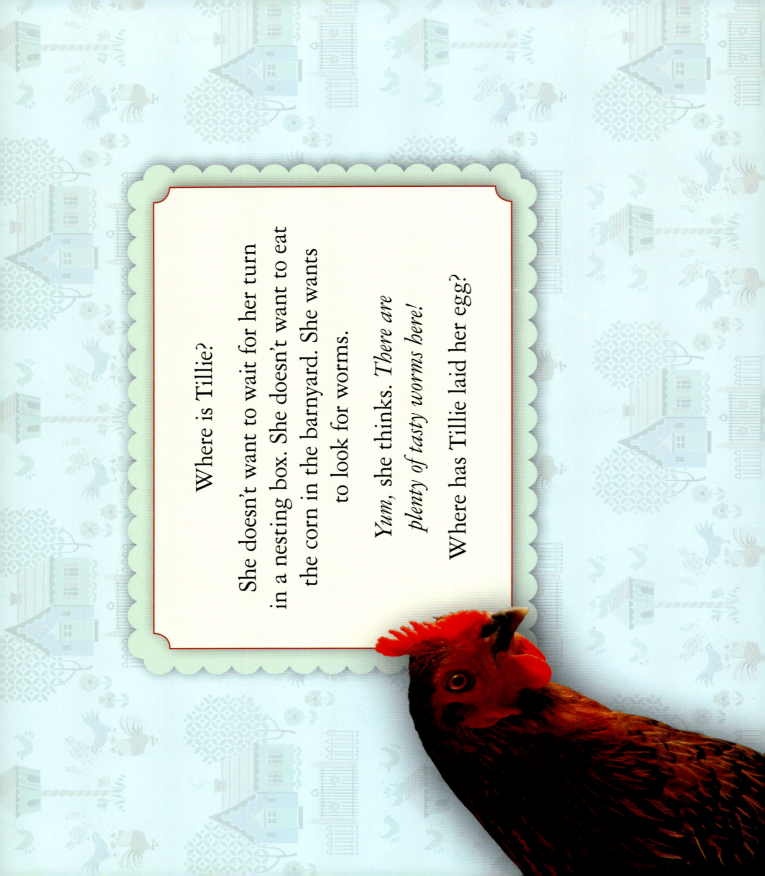

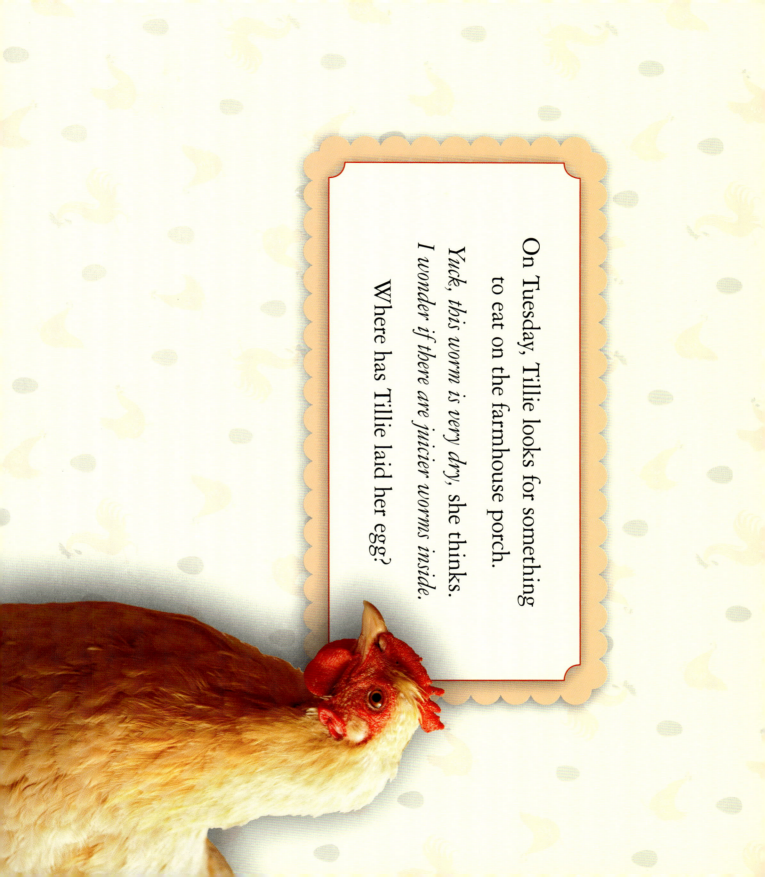

On Tuesday, Tillie looks for something
to eat on the farmhouse porch.

Yuck, this worm is very dry, she thinks.
I wonder if there are juicier worms inside.

Where has Tillie laid her egg?

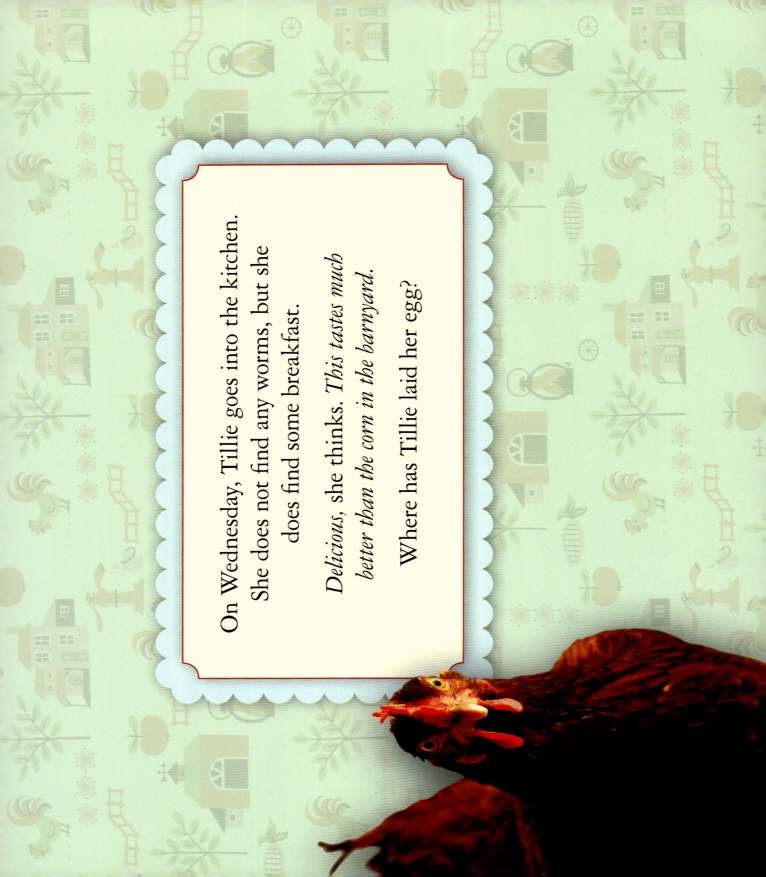

On Wednesday, Tillie goes into the kitchen.
She does not find any worms, but she
does find some breakfast.

Delicious, she thinks. *This tastes much
better than the corn in the barnyard.*

Where has Tillie laid her egg?

On Thursday, Tillie goes into the laundry room.

Ahh, she thinks. *What a cozy nest. Time for a nap.*

Where has Tillie laid her egg?

On Friday, Tillie explores one of the bedrooms.

Hmph, she thinks. This place has everything but worms.

Where has Tillie laid her egg?

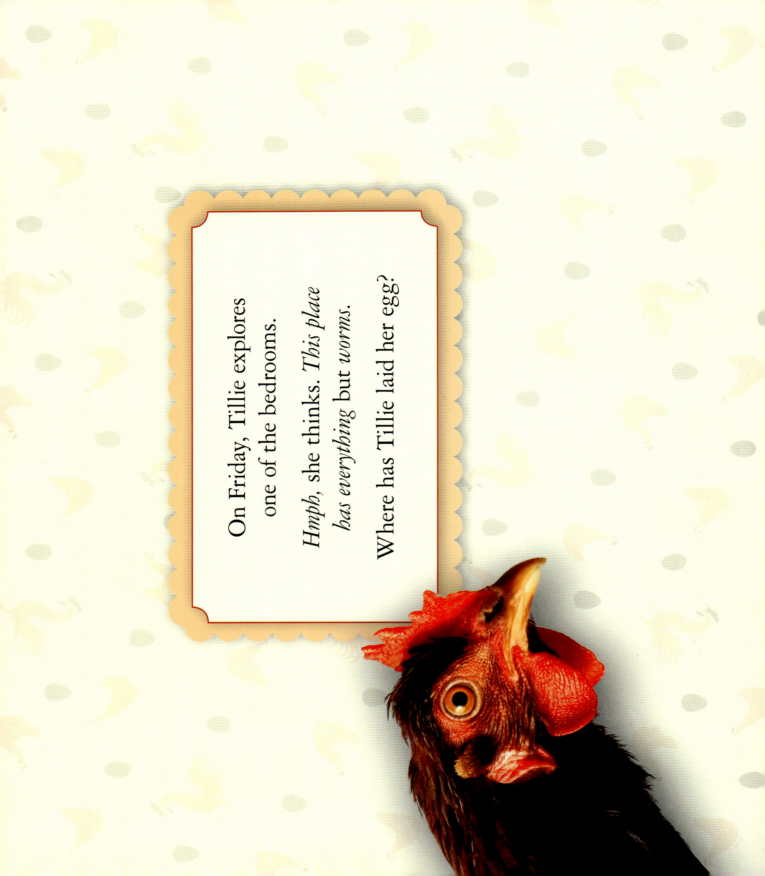

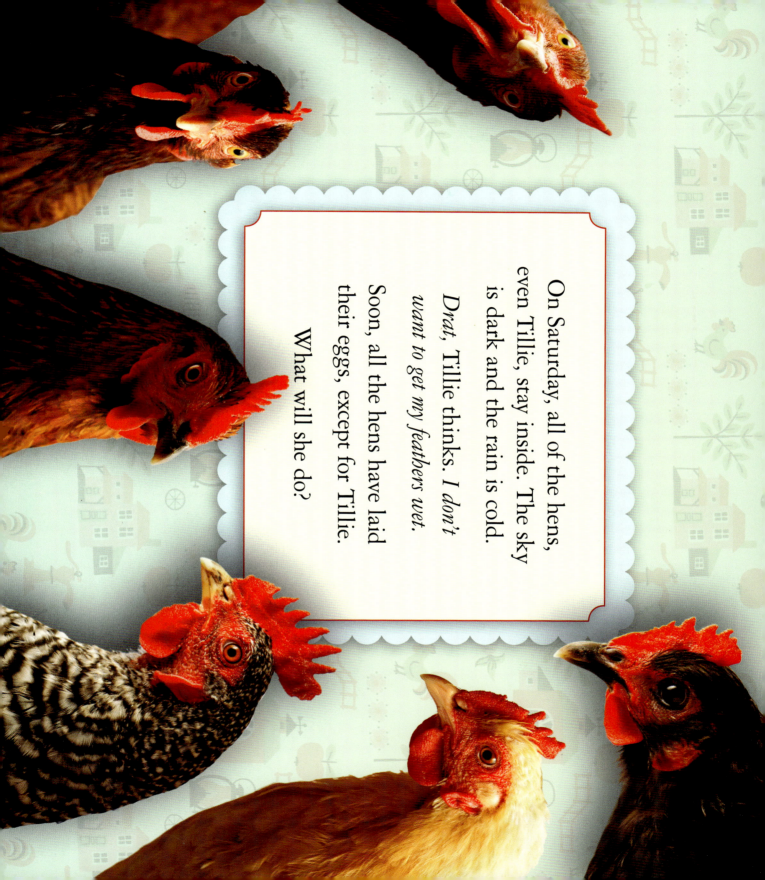

On Saturday, all of the hens, even Tillie, stay inside. The sky is dark and the rain is cold.

Drat, Tillie thinks. I don't want to get my feathers wet.

Soon, all the hens have laid their eggs, except for Tillie.

What will she do?

Tillie hops up and looks inside a nesting box.

Mmmm, she thinks. This nest is warm and dry. And very comfy.

Finally! cluck the other hens. Tillie laid an egg!

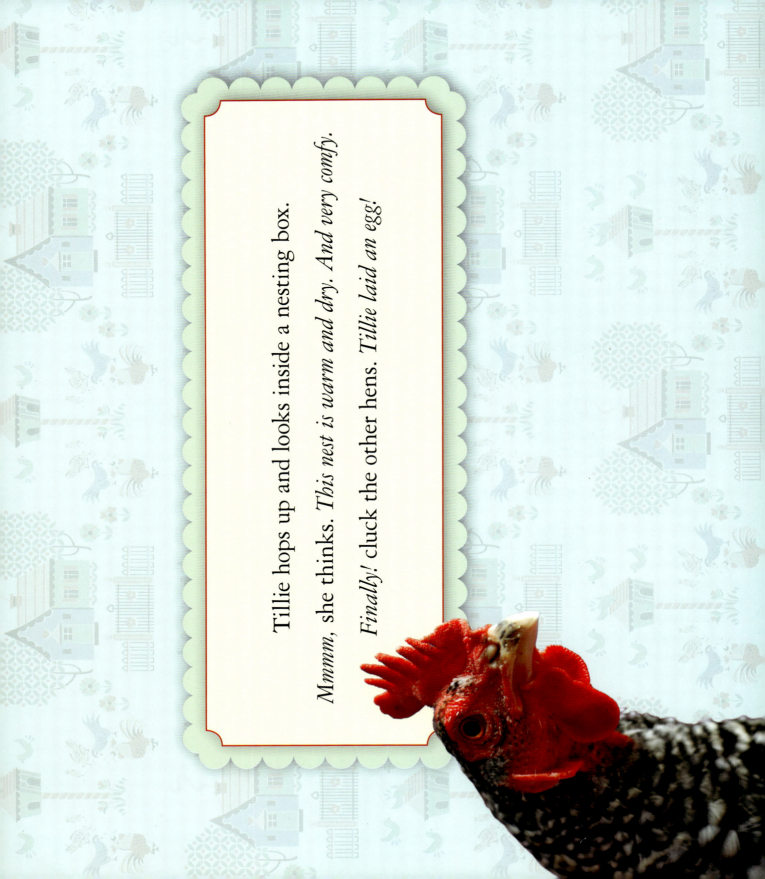

On Sunday, Tillie peeks outside.
The rain has stopped.

Look, look, she clucks.
Worms are wiggling in the dirt!

The other chickens don't notice.
They are too busy scratching for corn.

You don't know what you're missing!
thinks Tillie. Off she goes!

Where will Tillie lay her egg today?

A Note from the Author

All of the hens that appear in this book live in my backyard. The girls were (and are) treated eggs-tremely well – in fact, they were given too many treats during the photo shoots and now they are quite spoiled and demanding. Tillie is a special hen and the inspiration for this tale. She took to the photo sessions with her characteristic chipper aplomb.

The props used in the book all come from my private collection. The only item I don't own (but wish that I did) is the red pickup truck, which was lent by Marjie Findlay. Pagey Elliott cut the jigsaw puzzle seen in the bedroom tableau.

I owe a lot to my mother, the late Lois Blonder who, at an early age, introduced me to flea markets.

I couldn't have done this book without Ben Fink. Ben is a genius behind the camera, and a fine friend. I could say more, but he's heard it all from me before.

It's a cliché to thank one's spouse for everything, but I will. Steve keeps the HenCam working and my heart warmed.

—Terry